DOT

LAWRENCE SIMPSON

ISBN: 978-1-7330446-6-0

DISCLAIMER

This is a work of fiction. No aspect of this story depicts real persons living or dead. Any similarity is coincidental. The use of place names is entirely fictional.

For my Family

CHAPTER ONE

Lance Kenyon woke up empty. Dawn drifted through his bedroom window, and the absence of darkness pulled at his senses. He rubbed the last pleading images from his eyes.

He swung to sitting on the side of the bed before getting up and padding into the bathroom to wash his face and shave. He turned the hot water spigot and waited a few seconds before splashing his face. He reflexively held his breath as frigid water reminded him that he still hadn't picked up a new thermostat for the water heater.

He had laid out his clothes last night out of long-engrained habit. His oatmeal sat ready in a bowl on the kitchen table, and his tea bag hung over the rim in an empty cup. The whistling kettle of steaming water turned both into something life-sustaining. He stared at the steam rising from his teacup, and his mind chugged like a powerful train down a familiar one way track that always seemed to lead to the same question.

One year. That's how long since he had seen Alyssa. He dreamed of her often as he saw her the first time, cascading blonde hair framing blue eyes and white teeth that teased him whenever she spoke. That time she jumped into the water below the falls with her clothes on just to dare him. The way she smiled, her laugh, and the way she felt in his arms.

Every night he worried over what could have happened to her. He would imagine her overturned car, alone in the brush except for visiting wildlife. Last night, he wrestled in his special hell dreaming that she lay hurt, calling for him over and over.

God, he felt tired. The truth was that he returned home and couldn't find her. Her car and purse were gone. Nothing disturbed at the house. Her clothes still present. Her cold cup of tea sat on the kitchen table. There was no trace of her. Gone.

He held hope for months while he looked for her. He tried everything he had learned in his previous work. He called old friends, acquaintances, and people he barely knew. Anyone or anything he thought could help. But it was all for naught.

He rubbed both hands through his short brown hair, pushed back his regret, and pulled on his boots before heading out to the barn. Alyssa had loved animals, especially horses. Blaze whinnied a greeting to him when he opened the barn door. Their small barn held four stalls for horses, with an area for saddles, tack, tools, rope, and blankets at the back. The framed wooden walls to the right sheltered bags of feed and offered storage for hay. The earthy woodsy smell always made him think of happier moments when he and Alyssa worked side by side and dreamed of what they wanted together.

The gold colored stallion with a creamy white mane had found his way to her on their first anniversary. Alyssa and Blaze had bonded from the start. She loved the palomino saddle horse and used to ride him around their modest twenty-acre farm most every day. With her trim figure and bouncing blonde hair reflecting the sun, they made a striking pair.

Lance let the eager horse out of his stall and led him into the west pasture. He forked some hay onto the ground inside the fence and checked the trough to be sure there was enough water. Blaze would be content to graze there in the field for the next few hours.

I should find a home for him, he thought, but he wouldn't. It felt like a betrayal. Lance knew he wasn't taking care of Blaze well enough. One by one he had found homes for the chickens and the goats. Even the cat had run off. Another thing to feel guilty over.

He closed the barn and got in his Chevy truck with his lunch pail. Eleven miles away, he pulled into the feed store gravel lot and parked in the back next to the large storage barn for the store. Spring planting season had started, and it would be busy.

When Henry called two weeks ago and asked him to help for a few weeks, Lance almost told him no. But, he admitted, it felt good to get away from the farm for a few hours.

Henry's Feed Store was a landmark business in the area. The original building started as a general store in the late eighteen hundreds and had expanded several times. The original one story building made of slabbed pine logs stood surrounded on both sides by hardwood framed additions offering garden and farm tools and small engine repair.

Lance walked in to find Henry standing at the counter working with old man Martin on a grain purchase. Henry's steel blue eyes hinted at his stubborn nature. Close cropped white hair and gray stubble framed his serious face.

Frank Martin looked at Lance and nodded ever so slightly. Streaks of gray feathered his short sandy hair which threaten to climb back up his forehead. The slight bulge of his plaid shirt at the waistline gave testament to his years and hinted at the daily toil which kept it in check.

Lance nodded back and checked the tally sheet posted on the wall behind the counter. Henry had help in the afternoon from two local high school seniors, but in the morning during the week, it was up to Lance. He found the keys to the forklift and retrieved a pallet of Frank's preferred brand feed. He just managed ahead of the old cattle farmer, who three pointed his pickup and backed his hauler up to the loading dock like he had done it a thousand times before. Lance loaded the double axle utility trailer.

Frank put his receipt copy of the purchase order in his wallet. He hesitated, cleared his throat, and said, "Got a favor to ask. Wondering if you might help me unload this evening?"

Lance realized that might have been the first time he had heard the old farmer speak. It took a moment for the words to sink in. The Martin cattle farm was just around the corner from his place. Their pastures touched down by the small creek bordering their properties.

Lance said, "Sure. I can help you. What time?"

The old farmer looked a bit embarrassed but plunged ahead. "Thinking five o'clock. Still have some light to see by." He looked at the load on the wagon. "About an hour should do it." He held his gaze waiting for an answer.

Lance said, "I'll be there at five."

Frank nodded his thanks, climbed into his pickup truck, and eased out from the loading dock towing his grain load. Lance watched him drive from the feed store lot out to the county road and make a right turn to head toward town.

Henry emerged from the store's back door. "Did Frank talk to you about helping him this evening?"

"I told him I could," said Lance.

"Good," said Henry. "He ain't been the same since Patty passed."

Lance looked down at the ground and back to Henry. "I guess none of us have."

Henry nodded in agreement. "Would you check on the horses?"

"Sure," replied Lance.

Henry had a riding stable with half a dozen horses for people to rent in the summer. Except for Storm. The coal black mare let everyone know that she was Henry's horse.

The riding stable was painted fire engine red with white trim and visible from the road. There was a walking ring and gated corral fencing that allowed the horses to pasture on the ten acres behind the barn. Lance saw that the horses were already out for the morning. He filled the water troughs with a hose and pulled a bale of hay from the sheltered storage alongside the stable. He cut the twine around the bale and dumped it in the feeder station inside the fence which drew the horses.

Lance had never been on a horse in his life before Alyssa found him. She taught him to ride on all of these horses except Storm, but even though he hadn't ridden the midnight black mare, he had bonded with Henry's horse through Alyssa. Storm seemed happy to see him and thrust her nose at him demanding affection.

"I miss her too, girl," said Lance.

He continued baby talking with Storm and the other horses while doling out oats and hay. He knew Henry would have help from the teens in the afternoon to clean out the stalls before they went home. He thought on his conversation with Frank while he worked.

In the two years since he and Alyssa bought their place, he had seen Frank Martin all of four times and never exchanged more than a friendly nod or wave with him, but Alyssa had grown close to Frank's wife, Patricia, and visited with her often until last year.

Patricia Martin veered into a tree on a misty rainy day. She had been on her way home and just around the corner from their farm when the accident happened. Frank had been devastated.

Lance had been out of town that horrible week. Alyssa attended the funeral and called Lance that night in her grief. He had tried to comfort her over the phone.

I should have gone over to check on him, thought Lance. But Alyssa had gone missing, and after awhile, he had found it difficult to get out of bed. Still, Frank Martin was his neighbor.

Lance finished with the horses and found plenty of orders to fill when he returned to the feed barn. He stayed busy loading hay and grain and fertilizer. He finally had time to eat his sandwich around one o'clock when both high school teens arrived to help cover the afternoon.

Lance ate at the picnic table behind the store. He planned the rest of his weekend chores. He needed to pick up supplies and put in the garden at home, if he wanted to eat this year.

Besides, if he kept himself busy, he could almost pretend Alyssa was away on a trip. She might drive over the horizon, wind down the road, and come back to him. Anything was possible.

The back door of Henry's Feed Store opened. Deputy Wayne Stevens sauntered down the wooden steps and swaggered over to where Lance sat. The deputy stood medium height. He carried a stocky build and sported a smooth face that looked too young to take seriously.

"Henry says you have been here all morning," he said. "Where were you last night?"

Lance tried to ignore the deputy, but he knew the man would not let it go. Wayne Stevens thrived on being right and being the last one to speak. It hadn't taken Lance two minutes to figure that out the first time he met him almost three years ago.

Lance had stepped off the bus in Two Falls with all he owned in his utility bag. The connecting bus wouldn't be through until the morning. He had walked through town asking where he might find an inexpensive room for the night. Turned out there was only one place in town, and that was full. He had resigned himself to sleeping out overnight, even though the sky looked like rain.

Deputy Stevens had spotted him standing with his bag over his shoulder and interrogated him for ten minutes. Lance calmly answered his questions, but that didn't seem to satisfy the young deputy. For a moment, Lance thought the deputy meant to arrest him.

Alyssa had walked up to both of them and introduced herself to Lance. She said hello to the deputy and inquired after his mother. She smiled the whole time. Somehow, she just seemed to take control of the conversation. Deputy Stevens stuttered when he answered her almost like he was surprised she was talking with him. When she found out Lance was new in town with no place to stay, she thanked Wayne for looking out for a visitor and invited Lance to join her in the cafe to meet her father, Henry.

Entranced, Lance had followed her into the cafe and sat before her and her father like an empty cup waiting to be filled. He said little, but that hadn't mattered. Henry poured coffee for him from the carafe on their table, smiled at his daughter, and talked with Lance like he'd known him all his life. He offered him work at the feed store and a place to rest in a room over the feed store garage. The whole time Alyssa had beamed at Lance from across the table like a second sunrise.

Lance remembered the sour look on Wayne Stevens' face as Alyssa escorted him into the cafe that day, and Wayne didn't look much different now.

"Buying feed in your uniform, Deputy?" he asked. His question brought a flush to Wayne's face.

Before the deputy could speak further, Sheriff William Pullman stepped around the corner and called out to his deputy, "Have you found out anything?"

Wayne started to respond, when Matt Ralston, one of the high school boys walked up and interrupted. "Lance, we just got Wade Kocher in with his spring order," he said. "Could you give us a hand?"

Lance told Matt he'd be with them in a moment, then turned back to the lawmen and asked, "What's this about?"

"Girl went missing over in Flores Lindas yesterday evening," said Sheriff Pullman. 'Their police chief requested we ask around." The tall and weathered sheriff pulled his hat off and rubbed a hand through his gray hair.

"I was just questioning him," said Wayne.

The sheriff put his hat back on and faced his deputy.

"Did you find Ronnie?" he asked.

"No, he wasn't at his trailer," said Wayne. "No one's seen him in a day or so."

"You show Lance the flier yet?" asked the sheriff.

Wayne produced a piece of paper with a color photocopy of a photograph. Marta Janssen, age fourteen, blonde hair, full of life and smiling. The details on the handbill suggested she'd been missing since late yesterday afternoon.

Lance looked at the happy face in the photograph and tried to breathe. He felt like he was falling. Her sweet smile reminded him of Alyssa and pulled him deeper into the abyss his life had become.

He rolled up his napkin and closed his lunch pail. "I was at home last night,' he said. "I have not seen her. I'll keep an eye out. Good day, Deputy. Sheriff."

He nodded to both of them and went to help the boys finish loading one large order after another. Loading feed and hay bales led him to happier memories of stocking the barn at home for Blaze and how excited Alyssa had been.

He let the warm afternoon sunlight insulate him from thoughts of lost girls, lost love, and lost chances.

CHAPTER TWO

Lance pulled into Frank Martin's gravel driveway. The gate was open, and he followed a slight incline around a low hill.

He saw an older clapboard home with a long spindle wrapped front porch. The house had been painted in white with green accents. The paint looked fresh. The mature trees were set back enough to offer shade, but leave little danger to the green metal roof if they fell.

Lance checked his watch and saw he was on time. He hated being late. He'd had to rush at home only bringing Blaze back in with the lure of some rolled oats and a fresh flake of hay. He'd washed off some dust from the feed store lot, spooled up the truck, and headed over.

Frank waited for him in the yard. The old man waved and said, "Thanks."

Lance got out of his truck and followed him to his barn.

Frank had backed his trailer into his barn next to the purpose built shelving where he kept his store-bought feed. The old farmer reached down and slung the first bag up and back.

Lance saw right away that it would make the job easier if he moved the bags back deeper, and he jumped up on the shelving to make that happen. One by one, they stacked the bags of feed with care.

To his surprise, Frank began to talk. "I been meaning to tell you how much I appreciated Alyssa coming out to the house when my Patty died. I was in a bad way then. She was uncommon kind, your wife."

Lance tried to swallow, but his throat felt like wood. He managed to say, "Alyssa loved to visit with Patricia."

Frank nodded his appreciation at the comment. They kept working. The old farmer never slowed. He set the empty pallets off to the side, likely with a planned use for them.

"Saw the sheriff's truck at Henry's on my way out of town around lunchtime," said Frank.

"There's a girl gone missing in the neighboring county," said Lance, lifting another bag of feed up on the growing stack. "Sheriff Pullman and his deputy showed us a photocopy and asked if anyone had seen her."

Frank didn't respond at first, but kept to his work. There were only a few bags left.

"Bill Pullman is a good man," said Frank. "Been the sheriff around here for a long time. He's talking about retiring later this year. Hate to hear that." Frank stopped and shook his head. "Girl gone missing, eh. Sometimes I just don't understand this world."

"Yeah," said Lance and nodded his head in agreement. "You know anyone named Ronnie?"

Frank looked up at hearing the name and said, "Why do you ask?"

Lance pushed another bag to the back of the growing stack.

"I heard the sheriff ask Wayne if he had found Ronnie," said Lance. "I just wondered if it was connected."

Frank removed his worn straw hat and wiped his forehead.

"Know of a Ronnie living over by the falls area in an old trailer," said Frank. "He worked for me for a few weeks about a year and a half ago, but I had to send him on his way."

Lance lifted another bag, slung it up on the stack, and began to push it back to make room for the next. They were almost done. He decided to go ahead and ask the obvious question.

"Why did you let him go?"

"Caught him drinking during working hours," said Frank. He winced and looked down at his feet. He twisted his hat in both hands.

"Worse, he tried to lie about it. Just too dangerous working a cattle farm with anything but a clear head." Frank put his hat back on and reached for one of the remaining bags and tossed it up on the stack. "He mouthed off at me some 'fore he left," he added. "Found out later from Bill that Ronnie had some history that I didn't want Patty to find out about."

"Sorry to bring that up," said Lance.

The old farmer just shrugged his shoulders.

Lance helped with the last few bags. He was tired when they had the trailer emptied. He walked out of the barn and headed over to his truck, thinking the deed finished.

"Well, uh, hold on there," said Frank. "I would take it kindly if you would come into the house for a moment. I got someone I want to introduce to you."

Lance did not fully understand, but he followed his neighbor as asked.

"Haven't seen you at church much lately," Frank remarked.

Lance didn't know what to say. There was no denying the observation from the old farmer.

"I've been feeling a little lost, I guess," said Lance. He couldn't believe he said that. He never shared his feelings with anyone since Alyssa, except maybe Henry.

"That's been known to happen to a man when he's lost his course," said Frank, nodding in agreement as they walked up his porch steps.

Lance entered the front door of Frank's house to find a waxed and shined hardwood floor with a carpet runner leading down the hall. To the left he saw a wall of books lining a sitting room. The hallway led to a dining room on the left and a kitchen in the back from which wafted a tantalizing aroma of something on the stove.

A feminine voice called out, "Is that you, Uncle Frank? Wash up. Supper's almost on the table."

Lance hesitated. Her words rang like a tuning fork. Memories stampeded. Wonderful, powerful memories so sweet he thought he would choke trying to rope them back under control. He did not need to break down in front of this old man and his niece.

"Laura, this is our neighbor, Lance Kenyon," said Frank. "Lance, this is our niece, Laura Wells. She's just arrived to stay with us for awhile." Frank still spoke as though Patty were standing beside him.

Lance had expected a younger woman from her voice. She looked to be closer to his age, fair haired and fair skinned.

Laura smiled and said, "Hello. I didn't know Uncle Frank had anybody else here."

"I didn't mean to intrude," said Lance. "You and your uncle need to sit and eat. I'll see myself out." He spoke to be polite, but her blue eyes gathered him in. He couldn't look away.

Her lips moved and words sang out. "Nonsense. You've both been working, and we all need to eat. Wash up and sit down. We've enough for three." And that was that.

Lance washed his hands and tried to make himself comfortable. He couldn't remember the last time he'd dined with anyone else. That wasn't true though, and he reminded himself not to lie, even to himself.

The table, now set for three, sported fresh cornbread, spring onions, lettuce, and a big bowl of beef stew steaming a heavenly fragrance. The three of them sat silent for a moment.

"Father in Heaven," prayed Frank. "bless this food, our lives, and our choices. All to your glory, Amen."

Laura echoed her uncle in their familiar meal time prayer.

The food tasted as good as it looked. Lance hadn't realized how hungry he was. He tried not to embarrass himself while he worked steadily at the stew.

"You live just north of Uncle Frank," said Laura. "Is that right?" She offered him some butter for his cornbread.

Lance thanked her and said, "We bought the place more than two years ago." He knew she was just being polite.

"We?" said Laura.

"Alyssa and I," said Lance. He looked away.

Frank ate deliberately.

"Alyssa is your wife?" asked Laura.

She looked at Frank who continued to concentrate on his food.

"Is she waiting for you to come back home?" asked Laura. "I should have asked. I'm sorry. I can be bossy, I know."

Lance realized she expected a response from him. "She's not at home. It's okay." He didn't want to explain. It always became real when he talked of it.

Frank took pity on him and said, "Alyssa disappeared about a year ago. Lance lives alone now except for that nice-looking horse." Frank turned to address him. "You ever think about selling that palomino, you come talk to me, hear?"

Laura set her lips together tightly. She looked at her uncle. Lance knew that look. Funny how women's eyes could be so full of words.

Lance had nearly finished his stew. He thought about asking for more. Before he could say anything, Laura ladled another spoonful into his bowl. Her hand trembled minutely.

"I'm sorry," she said.

He let himself examine her face for a moment. She held his gaze and seemed to be searching for something more to say. She looked away first, a slight flush to her cheeks.

"Thank you," he said and meant it.

Lance realized it didn't hurt him to acknowledge that to her.

He glimpsed Frank eyeing the two of them, but when he looked again, the old farmer was staring at his food.

"How did my uncle drag you over here this evening?" asked Laura

Frank jumped to answer. He explained how he'd seen Lance at the feed store, and since he needed some help to unload, he'd asked him to come over. The old man finished his explanation in one breath and helped himself to a second wedge of cornbread.

Laura's face turned quizzical. "I've not seen you need much help before," she said. She turned her attention back to Lance. "You work at the feed store?"

"Weekday mornings during spring," said Lance. "Henry asked me. He's a good man. It's keeping me busy."

He could see her thinking over his words. He knew she was probably trying to figure out how he could afford to work so little. His place wasn't much more than subsistence at best.

Lance knew someone else would tell her about the pending life insurance policy. Somehow the amount had spread itself around town. People were convinced he'd made millions tax free from his wife's disappearance. It was a sore spot with him. In reality, he had languished for the last year exhausting their dwindling savings account. Thankfully, she didn't ask.

"Church Spring Social is Sunday afternoon," said Frank. "Should be a nice time." He spooned more stew over his remaining cornbread.

"I hadn't thought about going, Uncle," said Laura. "I doubt anyone in town would remember me."

She spoke quietly, her hands resting together in front of her on the table. She glanced out the dining room window like she was seeing something far away.

Frank kicked Lance's leg under the table causing him to jump slightly.

"Well, I mean, uh, I guess I could introduce you to a couple of other people," said Lance.

Now why had he said that? He wasn't planning to go to that event. He hadn't stepped into church in months.

"Well, if you are going, at least I'll know one other person," said Laura. "You'll be there then?" She finished her words with a shy smile.

Lance nodded slowly. "Yes," he said, feeling like the first time he waded into deep water and struggled to stay afloat.

Frank smiled and ate his cornbread.

Lance finished his bowl of stew. He mentioned that he needed to take care of some things at home, thanked Laura for the meal, and said his goodbye.

Frank got up to go outside with him.

Walking out to his truck, Lance said, "Frank, I'm sorry about Patricia. I'm sorry I wasn't here."

Frank searched for words. Finally, he said, "Alyssa told me why you were out of town. We loved her, you know. My Patty thought the world of your wife."

Lance reached his truck and opened the driver's side door.

"Thank you for earlier," said Frank. "I'm all Laura has now."

Lance had one foot in his truck with his hand on the door. He looked at Frank and then down at the ground. He said, "You know what some in town think of me, right?"

Frank toed the gravel driveway with his boot. "Henry trusts you."

"Well, I married his daughter," said Lance. "There's that."

Frank nodded and didn't have to say more. Lance knew what he was thinking. Fathers loved their daughters, and uncles loved their nieces, too.

"See you Sunday," said Frank.

Lance closed his truck door and leaned out on his forearm. "See you then." He turned his truck around to head down the driveway.

Looking in his rearview mirror, he noticed Laura at the front door watching him pull away.

CHAPTER THREE

A curtain of misty rain from late afternoon clouds heralded Lance's turn from Frank's driveway onto the two-lane county road running in front of the Martin Farm. The drive back to his place was winding and just over a mile. He turned on his fog lamps and slowed down in the gloom and moisture, as asphalt tended to be slick just after a rain started.

He stopped at a T-intersection long enough to look both ways and started his left turn. The moment his foot pressed the gas pedal, he saw something in the middle of the road. He jerked forward in his seat as he slammed on his brakes. Just as he stopped, a ghostly gray van careened across the road missing the front of his truck by inches.

Lance gripped the steering wheel and willed himself to calm after his rush of adrenaline. Where did that come from? Had he seen headlights? The unknown vehicle had knifed through the gray gloom without even a ripple of tail lights.

The mystery shape in the road remained. Lance considered driving around it, but stopped himself. He couldn't live with the idea of someone having an accident.

He set his truck in park, made sure his flashers were on, and stepped out to investigate. He heard a slight whimper when he got closer. He saw now, through the fog and wet, that it was a medium-sized dog. It lay unmoving on the ground. He heard a whimper again. He could see blood high on a rear leg. He held his hands outstretched, palms forward, and approached until he stood over the injured animal.

He reached down and gently touched his hands to wet fur. The animal shuddered, but didn't snap at him.

"Hey dog, I won't hurt you," said Lance. "I'm sorry this happened to you. Did that mean old van hit you?"

He couldn't leave the injured animal here in the middle of the road. He sighed, knowing what he had to do.

"Gonna get you someplace warmer," said Lance. "Hang on now."

He carefully picked up the injured canine, hoping he wasn't making anything worse. The wet dog whimpered again but did not resist him. He found room in the jump seat of his truck and laid the dog on an old feed sack left over from work.

He carefully drove the rest of the way home in the darkening gray. Parking in front of the house, he heard a neigh from the barn.

"I'm home, Blaze," he called out. "I'm sorry. I'll be out with you in a moment."

Thinking to himself how Alyssa had spoiled the horse, he carried the injured dog inside and found a place by the wood burning stove in the kitchen. He built up a fire, and the warming glow filled the room.

He moved a lamp closer and inspected the dog he now saw was female. "Hey girl, let's see how bad you're hurt."

He found a tender area in the dogs left thigh. There was a cut, but he didn't feel any misshapen angle along the bone. "Hmmm, maybe it's not so bad. Let's get you cleaned up a bit."

Lance gathered a basin of water and a washcloth. He gently cleaned the laceration and applied triple antibiotic ointment. Her fur was matted and wet, and would have been mostly sandy brown colored if it weren't so dirty. Her head and face were the same tawny brown except for a small white patch in the center of her forehead. She needed a bath and a rubdown, but Lance didn't want to risk hurting her. It could wait till tomorrow.

"I'll call you Dot for now," he said to her. "because of that white dot on your forehead. I don't know your real name unless you want to tell me."

He continued murmuring to the animal as he tended her. He covered Dot with an old blanket.

"I'll be back. I have to go check on his highness."

Blaze pretended Lance wasn't there when he walked into the barn. The stallion's feelings bruised easily if he was left alone for too long. However, Lance brought a secret weapon with him. He held out his hand to reveal two fresh carrots.

Blaze whinnied once and clopped over to Lance. The horse eyed the carrots for just a moment, then deigned to bend his nose to one of his favorite treats. The stallion gobbled the carrots up while Lance rubbed the horse's ears and neck and told him how much he had missed him all day. Lance kept up a steady low murmur of conversation. He knew the stallion didn't understand all of the words, but he understood the emotions behind them and relished the attention.

While tending to Blaze, he thought over the day. He saw Laura sitting at the table and standing by the door. He thought of the sound of her voice...

And he felt guilty.

Lance shook his head. It was hopeless. It wouldn't be five minutes at the Church Spring Social before someone pulled her aside and asked about him, then gave her their version of his story: Lance hadn't grown up in Two Falls. He was an outsider who showed up one day and married one of the prettiest girls in town, scooped up a farm, lost his wife in a very suspicious manner, and kept to himself living off the insurance money. Yeah, that was the story, and it would go over really well with Laura. He needed to put his mind at rest about that.

He next thought about the missing girl and the look in Sheriff Pullman's eyes. The old lawman hadn't accused Lance of anything but seemed more hopeful, maybe, that talking to him would shed some light on the case since they were at a loss.

He knew the sheriff, of course. After Alyssa's disappearance, Lance had been in the sheriff's office almost daily for three months. Sheriff Pullman had asked him at one point if he wanted to take work as a deputy with the department. Lance had told the sheriff that he didn't do that kind of work anymore.

The deputy was a different story. Whenever he thought of Wayne, his mind flashed to a nature special about hyenas he and Alyssa had watched one evening together with Henry. Lance had mentioned the comparison, and that was the last time the three of them laughed together.

He took a curry brush in hand and rubbed Blaze down. Something the big horse dearly loved. He made sure there was fresh water in the buckets and placed a scoop of oats in the feed bin. He patted Blaze and told him good night. The big softy gave him a horse kiss on his face before turning to the oats.

Animals were so much easier than people, he thought. It had taken him months just to get back to any kind of function after Alyssa vanished.

Laura's face flashed through his mind again, but he pushed the image away. He wasn't ready. He just wanted to be left alone.

Didn't he?

CHAPTER FOUR

Saturday morning dawned clear and cool after the light rain overnight. Lance woke to birds chirping outside his bedroom window. A pair of meadowlarks had set up a nest in the tall grass just shy of the house. Their colorful whistles and warbles eased his mind into wakefulness. "Guess they got braver without that cat around," he muttered as he rolled over.

He and the cat never got along well. He had banished it to the barn where Alyssa would make sure it had food. Sometime after she was gone, it just wasn't there anymore.

Lance was finishing his shave when he remembered the dog. For a moment, he pictured walking into his kitchen and finding a stiff and still animal to bury. He rinsed off his razor, toweled his face, and padded down the hall. He peered beyond the kitchen door and saw a blanket covering muddy fur and a feathery tail that thumped up and down twice.

He pulled the blanket aside and saw Dot's big brown eyes looking back at him.

"Well, good morning to you too," he said.

A thump of tail hitting the floor answered him. He inspected her wound, which looked like it was already trying to knit back together. He would clean it again today.

"Listen girl, I've got to let Blaze out. I'll be back."

Lance made sure the stove was warming the kitchen and put the kettle on. He walked out to the barn and tended to the stallion, who was keen to be out and about. As he walked back up to the house, he was surprised to see a car pull into his driveway. When Laura got out, his heart beat a little faster.

"Good morning," she said. "I hope this is okay. I wanted to thank you for helping Frank yesterday. I would have called, but do you even have a phone?"

Lance smiled. He couldn't help it. She was right. He did live in isolation.

"You got me," he said. "Keeps the bill collectors away." He waited, not knowing what to say next, then he said, "I just put water on if you'd like some tea."

"Yes please," said Laura.

She reached into her car, pulled out a paper sack, and followed him into the kitchen which had warmed nicely. The kettle whistled a greeting. He got down another cup and turned to ask her how she liked her tea when he heard her exclaim.

"Oh my goodness. Who are you?"

He saw Laura kneeling next to Dot and stroking her matted fur, much to the delight of the injured animal.

Lance cleared his throat.

"That's Dot," he said. "At least that's what I'm calling her. I found her in the middle of the road last night, brought her home, and tended to her wound. She seems to like you well enough."

"She has no collar," observed Laura.

"I guess I could put a notice up at Henry's to see if anyone is missing a dog," said Lance. He told her about his near miss last night driving home.

Laura found two plates while she listened to him. She pulled out four big homemade donuts from her paper sack and portioned them on the plates.

Lance poured her tea.

Laura gathered herself in stillness for a moment, and he realized she was praying. She opened her eyes and said, "She's lucky you found her."

Lance had his mouth around a donut. They tasted as good as they smelled of butter, cinnamon, and brown sugar. He tried not to moan when he took the first bite. He managed to say, "Thank you."

She smiled, and the room brightened, or maybe a cloud passed, but something felt better.

"I need to wash her up and put more ointment on that wound," said Lance. "Guess I'll run her by Herb on Monday."

He explained that Herbert Hoover Boone was the local veterinarian.

He felt a wet nose against his hand. Dot stood beside him, slowly wagging her tail.

"Guess someone else likes donuts," he said.

Laura laughed.

Lance put down a bowl of water and placed some turkey from a pack of cold cuts in another bowl. Dot wolfed down the meat slices and lapped up the water. She looked at him with the imploring look he sometimes got from Blaze.

Next thing he saw, Dot had wrapped herself around Laura, or was it the other way around?

"Oh, she is sweet, Lance," she said. "Somebody must be missing her."

Laura looked around the kitchen. Lance noted her approval. He hated dishes in the sink and, though his standards had slipped some in the last few months, his natural tendency was neat and orderly. Another gift from his time with the Army.

"Thank you again," Laura said. "Frank would never admit it, but he is feeling his age lately. I'm worried about the work he has to do around the place."

Lance didn't want to pry but found himself curious. "You grew up here in Two Falls?"

"My mother used to bring me for visits," she offered. "I got to spend some great summers here, but I grew up in Reno." She hesitated for a moment, then said, "That is, until I lost my job there, and Frank offered me a place to stay."

"He seems like a good man." Lance didn't know what else to say.

Again Laura hesitated, this time much longer. She broke eye contact and, for a moment, Lance wondered if he had touched a nerve by asking about her past. He started to apologize for prying, but before he could, Laura sighed and said, "I knew Alyssa."

Lance grew still. Had he heard her right? He gripped the small table in the kitchen reassured by how solid it felt in his hands. There was little chance it would disappear behind his back.

"I stayed summers here. She and I were friends." Laura spoke carefully, unwrapping each word like a treasure. "We shared our secrets and our dreams."

Lance thought on her revelation and struggled to say, "I'm sorry. I don't remember Alyssa mentioning you."

Laura looked down.

"We hadn't spoken in years," she said. "My fault more than hers. We both had our lives, but she wrote me about you last year." Laura locked her eyes on his. "I should have told you last night at dinner. She loved you with all her heart and soul."

Lance felt the tears. He couldn't stop them. The hurt strangling his soul leaked out through his eyes and blurred his vision. He turned away, unwilling to let Laura see him like that.

He felt pressure on his leg. Dot had come over to sit beside him and raised her paw to rest on his knee. She rubbed her muzzle against his leg. Laura placed her hand over his and waited for him to come back from his dark place.

It must have been the tears in his eyes. The sun glinting off her fair hair almost looked like a halo. He had an angel in his kitchen, an angel who brought donuts. He smiled and said, "She saved me, you know."

"Alyssa was good at that," said Laura. She seemed like she would say more. Instead, she waited a few minutes and said, "I probably should get going. I promised Frank I would go with him to the hardware store."

Lance walked with her out of the house.

"What a beautiful horse!" she exclaimed.

A snort and a long neigh answered her. Before Lance could say anything, she approached the fence. In a few moments, she had Blaze licking her hands and nudging her to pet him.

"Oh, what a big beautiful baby," cooed Laura.

Lance had been about to warn her. Blaze was a sweetheart to people he trusted, but he tended to not like strangers. He had a bad experience with his first owner. Herbert had involved Alyssa, and just like that, they had a horse in their lives.

Since her disappearance, Lance had gone through the motions. He and Blaze had grieved themselves about to death until all they had was each other. He thought he would never see the stallion take to anyone else like Alyssa.

He felt a nose against his hand. Dot had followed them out into the yard and slowly stretched up on the fence to get closer to the horse. Lance just had time to worry the palomino would take alarm, but Blaze snorted and lowered his muzzle until he was very close to the dog.

Dot let out a quiet whine and licked the palomino right on his nose. Blaze snorted and pranced, but came right back down to Dot, who licked him on his nose again.

"Would you look at that?" said Laura. "You'd think they knew each other all their lives." She was looking at Lance while she spoke.

"Funny how that sometimes can happen," he replied.

Lance followed Laura over to her car and waited while she got in and started it up.

She rolled her window down. "I'll see you at Mass tomorrow," she said, smiling, and drove down the driveway.

Lance watched her drive away and wondered when he had agreed to attend church.

CHAPTER FIVE

Saturday afternoon found Lance outside the entrance of the discount superstore in the neighboring county. Flores Lindas was a town almost five times the size of Two Falls.

He had debated whether or not to bring Dot with him, but ended up leaving her at home on her blanket. He told her she needed to heal and patted her head. She seemed to understand and obediently curled up in her space by the stove.

He drove in for supplies to this superstore warehouse about once a month. He and Alyssa had kept to that pattern, and the memories comforted him.

He had his list. He had taken inventory over the last couple of weeks. He picked up rice, shelf stable milk, dried milk, flour, corn meal, bacon, salt, sugar, creamer, tea, and frozen vegetables because he liked the taste better. He also found some carrots and apples for Blaze and kibble and dog biscuits for Dot. He picked up various paper products. Approaching the checkout lane, he saw a wall of smart phones. He sighed, decided on a particular model, and placed it in the cart.

On the way out of the store, Lance walked past a bulletin board and noticed copies of the same flier shown to him by Sheriff Pullman. Once again, he noted the resemblance between the missing young girl and Alyssa. She could have been a younger sister of his missing wife. Now that he thought of it, she looked like Laura too. They all could have passed as family.

Lance felt the hair on the back of his head tingle. It wouldn't stop. He didn't have a lot of parental advice growing up, but one kinder woman had told him he had a fair head on his shoulders if he wouldn't stomp on the right ideas trying to grow. It was one of her favorite things to say.

He took a copy of the flier out with him and rolled his cart to his pickup. He tucked the flier beneath his belt and began loading the bed of his truck.

"Mister, would you open this for me?"

Lance looked to see a woman in a car parked in front of him holding a bottle of water out of her driver's window. He looked around. She looked harmless. He made sure his cart would not roll away and walked the few steps to her car.

She offered the bottle to him with another "Please," and he loosened the overly tight plastic bottle cap without difficulty.

"Thank you," she said.

The photocopy he had stuffed behind his belt fell to the ground. He stooped to grasp it before it got away from him.

"That's a terrible thing," she said, eyeing the flier as he picked it up. "That young Janssen girl done gone from this world. It's just awful what's going on nowadays."

Lance agreed with her.

He turned to finish loading his truck when he heard her say, "The law in this county needs to catch whoever is doing this. Don't you know that's the second young girl to go missing around here in the last six months."

Lance felt his neck hairs stand straight up. Something on his face must have alarmed the woman. She rolled her window up about halfway.

He hastened to reassure her and asked, "Did you say there was another girl missing?"

The woman looked surprised.

"Yes," she said. "You must not be from around here. A pretty girl, not twenty-one, named Mary Carson Gentry went missing about six months back. A storm of people went looking for her, but nobody's seen her. Her family goes to our church. It's just about killed them."

Lance thanked the woman and wished her a good rest of the afternoon. He finished loading his truck and put the frozen items in the cooler he brought with him. He pulled out his new cell phone. He hadn't used a computer in months, but he could still do a search. He found what he needed with little effort.

He gulped air as he sat in his truck and looked at the photos on his phone. He told himself he couldn't really be sure, but all the instincts from his previous life crashed in upon him. He felt lightheaded and his lips tingled. He realized he was hyperventilating. He pushed his breath out through pursed lips just short of whistling to slow his breathing pattern. His hands trembled. He thought of the little girl. He looked from the faces on his phone to Marta's photograph on the flier. He forced himself to think. The odds were against her, but she deserved every chance.

Lance knew it would take him about an hour to get back home. He could spare an extra thirty minutes. He found the local police station using his newly purchased cell phone and walked inside. He introduced himself and asked to speak with the Chief of Police.

The young woman at the receiving desk looked at him in disbelief. "The chief is off on Saturdays. You should make an appointment unless this is something pertaining to an active crime."

"Is there anyone else I can speak with?" asked Lance. "Is there a duty officer present?"

He guessed his last question caught her off guard. She hesitated, then said, "Yes, just a moment." She picked up her handset, hit an extension button, and spoke quietly into the phone.

Less than a minute later, a burly middle-aged man in a tired gray suit presented himself.

"Hello," he said. "I'm Detective Richards. And you are?"

"Lance Kenyon," he replied.

Lance noticed the detective's dense black eyebrows rise slightly at his name.

"I'm not allowed to discuss anything pertaining to an active investigation," said Richards.

"I need to talk with someone about the missing girls-" Lance started to say but was interrupted.

"Just what is your interest in this?" asked Richards. The detective directed his attention at Lance with laser focus.

"I just found out about the other missing girl in this county," said Lance. "Did you notice how much they look alike?"

Richards narrowed his eyes but said nothing.

"I did a search," said Lance. "Over the last three years, six girls have disappeared from counties within a two-hour drive, and they all look alike." Lance pulled his phone out and scrolled through the photos he had saved. "See, they could all pass for sisters."

The detective held up his hand and motioned with his fingers. "Follow me."

Lance followed Richards around the corner into a blue walled office. There was a framed photograph of Pinkerton and Lincoln at Antietam on the wall behind a simple wooden desk. There were cartons of case records sitting on the metal shelving to the left of the desk. He saw a large regional map mounted on a wall cork board adjacent to the shelving. Several pushpins had been placed in a circular pattern marking locations on the map.

Once seated, Detective Richards said, "All right, out with it. Why are you involved in this? Your name is familiar. It'll come to me in a moment. I can't remember who told me." He shook his head in frustration. "Tell me you're not a reporter," he said. "We were promised cooperation from the local news."

"I'm not a reporter-" Lance started to say.

"Wait, you're the guy whose wife went missing. Stevens told me about you. You used to be a cop, right?"

Lance forced his emotions down. The thought of Wayne Stevens talking about him with anyone made him smolder.

"Yeah, I used to be a cop."

The detective pressed a little harder. "Stevens told me he liked you for your wife's disappearance."

"Yeah, except I was out of town when she went missing," said Lance.

Richards nodded. "He told me that too. Couldn't shake your alibi."

Lance said nothing. He held the investigator's gaze.

"Look, I'm sorry for pressing you," said Detective Richards. "You know how it's done."

And Lance did know. He had done it himself in the past.

"We're aware of the other girls," said Richards. "We might be slow, but we're not stupid."

Lance took out a photograph of Alyssa from his wallet.

"That's your wife?" said Detective Richards. He sighed and looked up from the photograph to Lance. "How long now?" asked Richards, his eyes more forgiving.

"It's been a year."

Richards looked at the map on his wall and said, "Where do you live?"

Lance reached out slowly, took a push pin off the desk, and stuck it in the map. It was nearly dead center between the homes of the other missing girls.

He looked at Detective Richards and said, "I think the killer lives in Two Falls."

CHAPTER SIX

Lance found a seat in a rear pew at Saint Lawrence just after Mass started. He had not slept well, and, Blaze had decided not to cooperate this one Sunday morning. He felt grateful to find a seat, since there were only a few empty ones.

The small Catholic Church hosted good turnout most Sundays. He'd attended regularly with Henry and Alyssa before her disappearance. Both had been surprised and delighted to find he had been raised Catholic.

Lance thought of Mrs. Lasky again. She had been the one good memory from his childhood. He didn't know how he felt about it all, but that kind old lady believed in Jesus and the Church, and she had believed in him.

He had bounced in and out of foster homes only to land back at the state home when she found him. He still remembered seeing her for the first time. A tall woman with white hair, chocolate skin, and a straight back, she had asked to see him. She introduced herself and asked his name. She asked him what he wanted from life. He kept trying to figure out what she could want with someone like him.

He had tested her beyond any righteous person's endurance, but she only held onto him tighter. He finally realized she would not let go.

All the time she kept repeating the same questions to him. What did he want out of life? Who was he going to be? What did he think when he looked at himself in the mirror? Those were hard questions for a teen runaway with a troubled past. She told him there was one rule in her home. Never lie. Not to her and not to himself. Looking back, he only knew she was there when he needed her, and that had been enough for him.

Later, when she needed him, he had been too late.

The day he identified her body at the coroner's office had been the beginning of the end for him in Kansas City. He thought briefly on those events, shook his head slightly, and said a prayer for her soul.

Lance looked up and saw Henry midway in the congregation on the right where he usually sat. Frank and Laura were seated across the center aisle from Henry. He tried to focus on the Mass, but between his prayers, he kept returning to his conversation with Detective Richards.

Lance had left his old life behind, but not his brain. It was clear to him now. Someone had been preying on young women of a certain type, and his wife had likely been one of them. He had failed her just when she needed him most. Just like Mrs. Lasky.

He felt the guilt again. But he reminded himself one more time that a subpoena couldn't be ignored. His previous life had tracked him down in Two Falls.

Lance gathered himself on the kneeler and tried to keep his mind on his prayers, but those memories crested his awareness once again like a roller coaster inching along each creaking decision by clattering result until he inevitably faced the emptiness that always left him rushing down the same ride to remorse.

Sheriff Pullman had come out to deliver the summons to Lance. The sheriff had apologized to Alyssa for interrupting the two of them with his duty and seemed truly sorry. Later that evening, Alyssa told Lance that she had grown up with William Pullman as sheriff. Henry and Bill were good friends.

Lance had returned, under subpoena, to Kansas City to face further inquiry. Alyssa had wanted to go with him, but he asked her to

remain at home. He hadn't wanted her to be exposed to the conse-
quences of his previous life.

Early that week, Alyssa had called him long distance upset. She told
him about Patricia Martin's accident and said there was something else
she needed to talk about with him but not over the phone. Lance had
promised to return home immediately after the hearing finished Friday,
but the judge held the inquiry over until Monday. The district attorney
supervising the case had sensed political gain and sorely wanted to
ensnare him, but the small-minded man didn't have the evidence he
needed to convince a grand jury.

Lance left Kansas City just after the dismissal, but not soon
enough. Alyssa disappeared sometime between her phone call and his
return. Sheriff Pullman investigated but couldn't find a clue to her
disappearance. Lance had seen the sheriff age in front of his eyes
having to tell Henry that he had no answers for what happened to his
daughter. Lance had confessed the same, but Henry never lost faith in
him. He could only guess at why. Maybe it was because his father-in-
law saw his own pain mirrored in Lance's eyes.

There were never any answers until now. Lance had learned from
painful experience that if he asked the correct questions the answers
would present themselves. The problem had been that the answers
were seldom what he wanted to hear or see. He could feel that he was
heading in that direction again.

Standing for the Sign of Peace, he realized everyone near him had
moved far enough away to avoid reaching a hand out. He nodded to
Henry and Frank, who both turned to see him. Frank nudged Laura,
who smiled when she saw him.

And just like that, he felt better.

He tried to hold on to that feeling for the rest of Mass. He
followed others in the pews ahead of him to accept Holy Communion.
On the walk back to his pew, he kept his head angled down but examined the faces paying attention to him. He saw Laura smile at him
again. He noted other eyes looking at him with curious concern. Still,
Lance felt better. He should have returned to church sooner. Alyssa
would not have been happy with him missing Mass. He owed her more
than that.

After the Benediction, Lance waited at the back of the church.

Father Thomas found him and said, "I'm so glad to see you back. I hope you found some peace today."

Dressed in his white alb and sporting a jovial smile, it was easy to see why this parish priest was beloved in Two Falls. Lance hadn't seen Father Thomas but once or twice in the intervening months since the pastor had come by the farm to check on him.

"I've stayed away too long," Lance replied.

"But you're back now, and our day is brighter. Will we see you this afternoon?" asked Father Thomas.

Lance assured him he would. He stepped out into the yard in front of the church and looked for Laura. He saw her talking with Henry and Frank and other parishioners.

He moved to join them, but Deputy Wayne Stevens and Detective Richards interrupted him. Wayne smiled from ear to ear. Richards looked embarrassed.

"Lance Kenyon," said the detective. "I have a search warrant here for your house and property. I need you to come with me."

"The sheriff knows about this?" asked Lance.

Richards started to answer, but Wayne cut him off. "I talked with Sheriff Pullman this morning, and he gave his go ahead. I'm here to make this legal."

"I'd like to take my truck back home," said Lance. He dared a short glance, and Laura was watching intently along with Frank and Henry and much of the remaining congregation.

Deputy Stevens said, "No way."

Detective Richards said, "Okay, but I'll need to ride with you."

Lance walked to his truck with Richards at his side. He could feel the heat from the deputy's glare on his back.

Once they were seated in his truck, Lance thanked the detective and told him to fasten his seatbelt.

Richards held his words at first, but before they were out-of-town proper, he said, "I'm sorry about this."

The detective started to explain, but Lance interrupted him. "When you talked to your boss, he told you to put me on the suspect list and come search my place, right?"

Detective Richards mumbled, "Yeah, something like that."

Lance looked both ways before turning onto the highway out of town. "Don't sweat it. I would have done it differently, but basically, you're doing the right thing. You don't know me."

Richards looked uncomfortable. "Yeah, about that. I called a friend who works in Kansas City."

Lance glanced at him, but said nothing.

Richards went on, "He looked up a few things for me. I pretty much got your life history from him, at least most of what is written."

"Not that much to tell," said Lance. He focused on driving.

"Uh-huh," said Richards. "Foster care, honorable military service, police officer in line for detective. The facts stopped there, but the story is you went mercenary on a street gang after they murdered an elderly lady."

Lance kept his hands on the steering wheel. He didn't look at the detective.

"Who was she?" asked Richards.

"She was my foster mother for a while," said Lance.

Nothing was said by either of them for a mile or two. Lance slowed for the turn towards his place. In his rearview mirror, Deputy Stevens followed in his marked vehicle with his blues flashing. Like it was a parade.

Detective Richards looked thoughtful. Lance thought he was going to ask him about his wife's disappearance, but the detective confounded him.

"How did you meet your wife?" asked Richards.

"I went to arrest him," said Lance, surprised that he said anything. "Maria Lasky never hurt anything or anyone that I knew, but she wouldn't back down either."

"The gang killed her?" asked Richards.

"The leader of the Kings murdered her," said Lance. "Everyone knew it. But there was no proof. I wanted to bring him in and force him to confess."

"Let me guess," said Richards.

"He didn't want to be arrested," said Lance. "He and several of his gang tried to kill me."

Richards didn't say anything, but he gave a long look at Lance.

"It all went down bad," said Lance. "The administration tried to use me to make it go away."

Lance shrugged his shoulders and kept his eyes on the road. He felt lighter somehow. He had not talked about this to anyone other than Alyssa and Henry.

"So, you left town and wound up here?" asked Richards.

"I drifted, looking for any kind of reason for what happened," said Lance. "I was looking for work too when my money started running low. I'd only planned on spending the night in Two Falls waiting on the next bus."

He told Richards how Alyssa walked right up to him and introduced herself and got him away from Deputy Stevens.

"I don't think he's ever gotten over it," said Lance.

Richards laughed. "Oh yeah. I can see that."

Lance pulled his truck into his front yard and sat behind the wheel. "She introduced me to her father, Henry, in the diner. She made sure I ate. She kinda took over my life to be honest." Lance wiped his face with the back of his hand. "Must be some dust," he said.

Detective Richards watched him and said, "I know you're not the one we're looking for. I'm sorry about your wife."

Lance nodded. He looked up. Dot was guarding the front porch and growling at Deputy Wayne Stevens, who had gotten out of his duty car.

CHAPTER SEVEN

Lance pulled his truck into one of the few remaining spaces in the church parking lot. He was an hour late because of the search on his property. The Church Spring Social occupied the ball fields adjacent to the small gymnasium behind Saint Lawrence. He sat in the truck and stared at the crowd gathered around booths and tables without focusing on any one individual.

Detective Richards was intuitive and far sharper than he liked to let on. He had been polite but thorough. While Deputy Wayne Stevens stood to the side looking impatient, the big detective seemed to enjoy himself. He had been especially taken with Blaze, and the palomino surprised Lance again by nuzzling up to Richards like he was an old friend.

Lance had walked the detective around the house and barn and pointed to his utility vehicle. He started it up and the two of them slowly ran around the periphery of the farm. At the far end of the west pasture, there was a gate in the fence guarding an old trail that led off under a tree canopy.

"Where does that go?" asked Richards.

Lance shut off the utility vehicle and said, "This property used to belong to a mining company."

"You're kidding," said Richards.

"The road to the mine used to run right through here, but the mine played out more than a hundred years ago," said Lance. He started the utility vehicle and maneuvered around a shade tree inside his fence line. "The company went bust, and left the land fallow. Henry bought it cheap and let us build on it. He deeded it all to Alyssa. I guess I own it, now."

After running the detective around his property with his utility vehicle, the two of them sat in the living room talking. Dot seemed a lot happier with Deputy Stevens out by his car but padded over to the window from time to time and fretted over his presence. The rest of the time, she flirted with Detective Richards, who stroked her ears.

Richards noticed the gun cabinet and said, "May I?"

Lance nodded, happy with the man's politeness. He did have a search warrant.

The detective examined the Henry .44 caliber lever action rifle and fingered the Ruger .44 caliber single action revolver. "These are nice."

"They were a gift from Henry on our wedding day," Lance said. "Don't tell him I told you, but that old man is wicked fast at Cowboy Action Shooting. He's been trying to teach me, but I'm fairly hopeless." He pointed to the smaller Ruger 10-22 model. "The twenty-two rifle there was set up for Alyssa."

"So, Henry is the fastest gun around, huh?" said Richards.

"No, that title probably belongs to the impatient deputy outside. I hate to say it, but he is magic clearing a holster."

Richards put the weapons back in the cabinet.

"We will find out what happened to your wife," he said.

That had been the end of the search.

Lance had watched from his porch while Richards walked down to Wayne and told him they were leaving. The deputy turned beet red and said nothing in return. He just dusted his hat against his uniform trousers and opened his driver's door. Richards got in on his side of the cruiser, and just for a moment, Wayne's face went slack. He looked at Lance and flashed a small knowing smile.

The image of that smile faded, and Lance came back to himself sitting in his truck in the church parking lot. He gripped the steering wheel until his hands shook. He kept seeing the face of the leader of the Washington Street Kings. Lance had seen the same smile on that wannabe gangster's face before the gangbanger realized that justice had found him.

Lance startled at a knock on his driver's side window. It was Henry. Lance opened his door and stepped out of his truck.

"What happened?" asked Henry.

Lance knew he would have to tell him. He didn't want to explain it here, but he didn't see any way out of it. His father-in-law wouldn't be put off, and he had a right to know, maybe more than Lance did.

"They searched my farm, but mostly I talked with Detective Richards," said Lance.

"Why?" asked Henry.

He told his father-in-law what he knew and what he suspected. Henry took it all in like a dose of castor oil.

"So, there are other girls missing, and you think someone we know from around here has been taking women. Maybe took our Alyssa and... " Henry couldn't quite bring himself to say the rest.

Little by little, Lance and Henry had lost hope. They had talked it out. Sometimes people went crazy, but that just didn't track with Alyssa. They both knew something terrible had happened to her. Both of them loved her deeply, each in one of the best ways that a man could love a woman.

"I still don't have a definite answer," said Lance. "Just suspicions."

Henry put his hand on Lance's shoulder and said, "You've a good head and a good heart, Son. I know you'll find out what happened to our girl."

His father-in-law's face took on a gray hue, and the old man's eyes glinted like polished obsidian. Henry clenched his fist at his chest, began to look pale, and wavered a bit on his feet like he needed to sit down. Lance helped him walk a few steps to an empty seat at a picnic table beside the gym at the edge of the parish school's ball fields. He went to fetch Henry a bottle of water. When he returned, his father-in-law had disappeared.

Lance looked around for him and muttered, "Where did he go?" Henry was nowhere to be seen.

Maybe the news had been a little too much for the old man and he'd headed home. Lance thought about returning home himself. He had promised to show up, and he had. That was enough. He would check on Henry on his way home.

"So you came."

It was Laura. She stood behind him with a smile. Lance waited for her to ask him about his encounter with the police, but she didn't. That was okay with him.

"Sorry, I'm late," he said.

She was wearing the print dress he had seen earlier at Mass.

"You look beautiful," said Lance.

He winced inwardly. What was he doing?

Her smile broadened. "Why, thank you cowboy. Were you going to drink that water?"

She teased the water bottle out of his hand, opened it, and took a long drink. A little of the water dribbled out of the corner of her mouth onto her neck. He couldn't help but watch the drops find their way down to her blouse. She swirled her skirt back and forth, her blonde hair swinging from side to side.

"You look happy," said Lance. "I'm thinking Two Falls suits you."

She nodded. "I remember my summers here fondly. I thought it was because of my uncle. I realize now it was more than that. It's the people here. There's something honest about this place."

Lance would have agreed with her a year and a half ago. He still believed in part, but he knew that evil could exist anywhere, and it had found Two Falls, Colorado.

Of that, he was sure.

CHAPTER EIGHT

Standing in the afternoon sun with Laura almost made Lance forget his concerns. He wondered what to tell her but didn't get the chance.

"There he is," a voice sounded from beside him.

Lance turned to his right just in time to see a crazed man launch a punch at his face. He ducked around the man's swing and took control of him in a shoulder pin.

The late middle-aged man foamed at the mouth. Saliva flecked from his teeth and his face flushed the color of blood. He smelled of sweat, anger, and fear. The man's striped button down shirt pulled free of his belted trousers as he tried to squirm free, but Lance held him firm.

A frenzied woman with a tear-stricken face crowned by unruly light brown hair pushed her way through the growing circle of onlookers and screamed, "Let my husband go, you murderer!"

She clutched a young girl's jacket to her chest.

The surrounding crowd of parishioners and townspeople tried to process this. Their moon-wide eyes ringed all about in groups.

"Let him go, Kenyon."

Those words came from behind him. He recognized Sheriff Pullman's voice. Lance released his hold on his assailant, who slipped to the ground.

The man glared at him and rubbed his right shoulder with his left hand. His right hand tore at the grass beneath his fingers and balled into a fist. He clenched his teeth and spat out, "Where's our daughter, you monster?"

Lance saw the crowd staring at him waiting for a reply. Several heads nodded up and down, agreeing with the overwrought man who had attacked him. His suspicion about the man's identity was confirmed a moment later.

"Are you Bob Janssen?" asked Sheriff Pullman. He stepped between Lance and the angry man still on the ground holding his shoulder.

Lance noticed Laura being pulled back into the crowd by Deputy Stevens. The deputy was pointing back at him and talking to her nonstop. Lance wanted to call out to her, but didn't want to speak over the sheriff.

The man nodded yes to the sheriff. His emotions had temporarily robbed him of speech. Bob Janssen took a deep shuddering breath. He pointed at Lance and said, "I found out our police department searched that man's place this afternoon. I want to know where our daughter is, and he's going to tell me."

All eyes were back on Lance. The surrounding crowd pressed in, eager to see the unfolding drama.

Laura was no longer in immediate sight. Lance glimpsed her across the field, her arms folded. Wayne gestured with his hand toward the growing onlookers and back to her. Lance could only guess at what the deputy was telling her.

"That's right," said Sheriff Pullman, standing beside Lance and facing the Janssens and most of the crowd. The sheriff extended his hand to point at him. "We searched his place this afternoon and found nothing. Do you know why we searched his property?"

Lance could see the sheriff had them all listening, even the Janssens.

"Because he tried to help," said the sheriff. "Lance walked into the police station in Flores Lindas and asked about the case."

Someone in the crowd said, "What business does he have doing that?"

Pullman looked apologetically at Lance before he answered.

"Because he used to be a cop in Kansas City," said the sheriff. "He had an idea about the case and went to share it. This is what he gets for his concern."

Many in the crowd wouldn't look eye to eye with the sheriff after his statement. Bob Janssen collapsed, not caring if any saw his tears. His wife knelt down, and they held each other.

Lance's heart went out to both of them. They had to be out of their minds with worry.

Someone from the crowd said, "Is that right, Lance? You got some thoughts to share about this? What do you know?"

Sheriff Pullman nodded to him.

Lance hesitated, took a breath, and addressed the crowd. "I think the man who took Marta has taken other girls in counties all around us and has been doing it for years. I think he took my wife... I also think he lives in this town."

The crowd grew agitated at his words. They were gesturing and whispering to each other until someone asked, "Sheriff, is that true?"

"I can't be certain yet," said Pullman. "but he may be right."

Lance saw a look of quiet determination come over the men and women standing around him. Several of them bent down to help Marta's parents stand up. Others in the crowd reached out to reassure the Janssens and pray for them. Shouts of "We have to look for Marta," and "We have to search right now," came from the crowd. Those sentiments echoed until nearly two hundred people had one thought: to find the missing girl.

Sheriff Pullman knew better than to stop that wave. But he tried to shape it.

"All right, everyone," said the sheriff. "Get your woods clothes, food, water, and flashlights. No one goes off alone or in less than groups of three. Anyone who has a two-way radio bring it. No one searches anywhere without me knowing about it. We meet back here in thirty minutes to set up our search pattern."

The crowd dispersed with purpose as directed. People talked

among themselves, and those not directly searching volunteered to watch children. Several of the women in the parish guided the Janssens to a shady area. They offered them water and tried to comfort them.

Lance saw Laura appear beside the support group around the missing girl's parents. She took a long look in his direction and started walking toward him. Deputy Stevens was nowhere in sight.

Sheriff Pullman watched his town set out with no small amount of pride. Lance could see it on his face.

"Why did you stick up for me?" Lance asked the sheriff.

"You still have friends on the force in Kansas City that remember you," said Pullman. "Besides, Henry thinks the world of you, and I've never known that man to be wrong. If you're willing, I could use your help."

Lance nodded and followed Sheriff Pullman over to his Bronco. Laura caught up with them and stood to the side while the sheriff talked to him. Pullman reached inside his vehicle door and pulled out a map and an extra radio. He circled an area on the map around and behind Lance's farm including the woods next to the old mine.

"If you see anything, call it in," said the sheriff. "No hero stuff. No vengeance either. We need to find the girl. Finding the perp is secondary, right?"

Lance felt his body harden up. It was a familiar feeling. "Copy that," he said.

Pullman laid an object in his hand.

Lance felt the six points and knew what it represented. He looked at the Esplendoroso County Deputy Star. He had let emotions cloud his judgement in the past with terrible results. He had sworn to never again take on that role.

"Look," said Sheriff Pullman. "I think you're right. We need to find that girl, and I'm shorthanded. I've only got Wayne, and I sent him to pick up a guy named Ronnie Everett, who's of interest in this case, but that's on the other side of town. So far, we haven't been able to find him."

The sheriff took his hat off and rubbed his hand over his gray hair. He put his hat back on and held both hands out with the radio and the map.

"Even when Wayne gets back," said Pullman. "I'll have a couple hundred jumpy civilians running around town and in the woods looking for that girl. The word on you is that you were a good cop. I flat out need your help."

Lance took the offered radio and map from the sheriff's hands and said, "Okay, just until we find the girl."

Sheriff Pullman motioned Laura closer and put a hand on her shoulder. He turned his head to Lance and said, "Frank told me he could take a group to search the Falls area. I promised to look after his niece. Can you take Laura back on your way home?"

Lance looked at Laura to see if she had any objection. She stood quietly without a yes or no.

"Yes, I can take her," he said. "I need one thing though."

"What's that?" asked the sheriff.

Lance nodded toward the Janssens. "I need to borrow their daughter's jacket."

CHAPTER NINE

Lance drove towards home. He kept to the speed limit and his thoughts. Laura sat beside him. He noticed her glance more than once at the deputy star he had placed in a tray on his truck dash. He knew she had heard much of what the sheriff said to him. Likely, she had heard other strong opinions about him while in town. He knew she'd received an earful from at least one townsperson.

"Did Wayne convince you of anything?" asked Lance. He immediately regretted asking.

Laura said nothing at first. She broke her silence when they reached the highway out of town.

"I was almost married," she said.

"Almost?" asked Lance.

"He wasn't who I thought he was," she said.

He glanced at her, nodded his head in understanding, and returned his attention to driving.

After a few minutes, she said, "Those poor people. I'm praying for their daughter."

He nodded in agreement.

"Lance?" said Laura. She kept her eyes straight ahead.

"Yes?" he replied, keeping his eyes on the road.

"He gave up on us," she said. "He gave up on me."

Lance dared a glance at her and said, "I'm sorry."

He negotiated the intersection for the county road leading to the Martin farm. The same spot in the road he had found Dot a lifetime ago.

Laura kept her blue eyes glued to him. He could see her at the periphery of his vision.

"You've never given up on Alyssa, have you?" she asked.

Lance slowed for the entrance to Frank's farm. He crept into the driveway and put his truck in park.

"It's just not in me to give up once I'm set." he replied.

"Wayne doesn't think much of you," she said. "He tried to warn me about you. He used to say all sorts of things to Alyssa and me when we were younger. We pretended not to listen."

Laura placed her hand over his and said, "My uncle thinks you're a good man, and Henry sets the moon by you. Sheriff Pullman seems to trust you."

Lance dared to turn his eyes toward her.

"Please be careful," she said. "If it comes down to you or the man that took that girl, make sure it's him."

Laura released his hand and climbed out of his Chevy. She walked up the steps, across the porch, and looked back at him before going inside.

Lance looked down at his hand for a moment. He put his truck in gear and drove back home. His mind kept flashing to memories of Alyssa and how he missed her.

And then he thought of Laura sitting beside him in his truck and the feel of her hand on his.

Dot waited for him on the porch, wagging her tail. She had healed quickly over the last two days. Lance could rub her flank without her flinching at this point. He gave her a good rub and told her to go fetch Blaze. He didn't know if she knew all his words, but she knew the horse's name.

The shepherd ran over to the pasture fence and barked twice, then twice again. Lance saw the palomino wheel and trot over to the fence next to the barn where Dot waited. Lance shook his head.

"You'd think the dog fed the big baby," he muttered.

He walked inside and grabbed two energy bars and his canteen. He buckled on his holster rig and tied it down. The loaded revolver found its way into his holster without a second thought. He loaded the Henry rifle and made sure his belt loops were full of extra cartridges.

He closed up the house and walked to the barn where Blaze waited. The stallion quivered his pleasure, expecting to go for a ride.

Lance looked over the search grid on the map again. The sheriff had tasked him to search the area of the county he knew best. The area around the mine stretched beyond his property and wound around the backside of the mountain. There was little in the way of access other than the over grown road from his place and a hard to ride trail around the back side of the mountain. Searching by horse made the most sense.

He grabbed a flashlight he kept in his truck and the sheriff's radio and placed both in his saddlebag. He waited a moment, grimaced, and pinned the deputy star to his shirt. He pulled out Marta's jacket. Her mother had passed it with trembling hands to the sheriff and confirmed her daughter had worn it the day she disappeared.

Lance closed the barn door. Dot sat with her tail thumping and gave him a look that said she would not be left behind on this adventure. He wondered if the intuitive shepherd would understand? He held out Marta's jacket to let Dot have a sniff.

"This is who we have to find, girl."

Dot's ears perked up and she tilted her head from side to side, listening to him intently. She barked once. Did she understand him? Sometimes, Lance thought, you have to go with your instincts.

"C'mon then," he told her, and she jumped to stay beside them.

The three of them cantered off toward the back of the property in a slow loping cadence. He kept Blaze in check. The palomino wanted to run, but Lance reminded the horse in calm measured words that they might be out all night. The spirited horse slowed to a steady walk.

Dot ran ahead and, now and then, put her nose to the ground. She didn't range too far or run away.

Lance felt a quickening urgency in his gut. His instincts told him that, somewhere in this county, a frightened and traumatized teen girl lay waiting for a miracle. He had seen similar cases in his former life as a cop. He knew the chances of finding her alive were slim. Just like Alyssa.

In the first few days after discovering his wife missing, he had trembled before almighty God bartering his life for her return. God's answer had been silence. As the long nights stretched to endless bitter months, that part of him Alyssa had nourished withered bare to fossilized rock leaving him hollow, heavy, and unmoving in the dark.

Mrs. Lasky had promised him that God hears all prayers. He could hear that old woman now.

"God may answer yes or answer no, but sometimes his answer is to wait in silent obedience," she said. "That's when you pray for understanding."

Every time he had given up, he heard that caring old woman whispering in his ear, urging him on. He prayed a new prayer that he might find Marta alive.

Please God, let me save this one.

Up ahead, Lance saw his fence gate straddling the old mine road. He had placed a stout padlock on that gate in the first few months of living on the property after seeing local teens trespass almost at will. They had grown used to riding their dirt bikes and ATVs up the trail and down the back side of the mountain.

The legend of the Switchback Mine remained standard fodder for young people in and around Two Falls. There were some who believed there might still be gold to find in the bankrupt mine. Many considered it community property, but Lance's name was now on the deed. He knew the fact that he owned the mine and the surrounding land irritated the locals since many still considered him a suspect outsider. It had made it harder to deal with trespassers. Approaching closer, he saw the chain hanging half off the gate. Someone had cut the padlock, and it lay on the ground.

He opened the gate. All was quiet except for squeaky hinges. Dot scrambled through the open gate. Blaze snorted and waited for Lance to climb back up after he closed the gate. This part of his property sloped up gradually, transitioning from grass to rock broken by conifers and persistent shrubs. What was once a dirt road had overgrown to a choked off trail.

Once in the trees, Lance saw some broken twigs here and there on the easier side of the trail. Looking ahead, he saw Dot sitting under an encroaching tree branch with her tail wagging back and forth. She sniffed at something in the tree branches and circled to sit again, her tail thumping the ground.

"What did you find, girl?"

Lance saw a scrap of torn fabric clinging to the sticky end of a ponderosa pine branch. He reached down to pat her head and said, "Good Girl."

Dot shivered in response to his praise.

The flier on Marta said she had last been seen wearing her school uniform jumper. The plaid fabric scrap was dark green with interwoven light green.

Lance checked the load on his revolver and chambered a round in the Henry rifle, carefully lowering the hammer against the transfer bar. If he needed it, he would only have to cock the hammer. He pulled the sheriff's radio from his saddlebag.

"Lance Kenyon for Sheriff Pullman," he said. It took two tries.

"Pullman. Go ahead. Over," responded the sheriff.

"I found a fragment of school uniform on the old trail up to the mine from my place," Lance said.

"I can't get over to you for at least an hour," said the sheriff. "I've got townsfolk scattered all over. I haven't been able to reach Wayne either. I'm worried."

"Copy that," said Lance. "Sheriff, I need to keep looking. If she's out here alive, I can't wait."

Pullman told him to be careful. He added, "Lance, you do what you have to do. I'll get out to you as quick as I can."

"Copy that," said Lance. "Oscar-Mike."

Lance put the radio away in his saddlebag. He adjusted his seat in the saddle. Blaze took a step or two. He patted him on the neck and said, "C'mon boy, let's keep looking."

The big horse stepped off up the trail with Dot running ahead, her nose in the air sometimes and on the ground at others. The shepherd stopped now and then to look back and make sure they were following.

The trail inclined in switchback after switchback. Lance knew this road once accommodated horse-drawn wagons. Those days were long gone without a tremendous amount of cleanup work.

In a depression on one side of the road around a clump of bushes he saw some tire tracks in damp pine needles mixed with old leaves and dirt suggesting an ATV had been up this trail since the last rains. He tried to remember when that was.

He was getting close to the old mine when Blaze flicked his ears. Lance heard a muffled sound up ahead and pulled the stallion up for a moment to listen. His nose filled with the scents of vanilla and butter-scotch from the ponderosa pines lining the trail along with saddle leather and sweat as he stood in his stirrups and strained to hear beyond the guarding evergreens.

He listened for any clue but only heard the murmur of swaying evergreen boughs conferring with each other in a late afternoon sigh of wind.

The trees kept any answers to themselves.

CHAPTER TEN

Lance studied the entrance to the old mine. The timbers at the front bore evidence of decay from weather and termites. His warning signs to ward off curious teens still hung to either side. The three-quarter inch plywood barrier door he had placed over the mine stood ajar in the late afternoon quiet.

Dot sat by his side. She looked ahead and softly whined. The Sun had given way to clouds, and the filtered light cast doubtful shadows in front of the mine entrance.

Blaze snorted behind him. Lance heard an answering neigh from his right through the trees. He secured the stallion and told Dot to stay, then pulled his revolver and crept through the brush to find a saddled black mare. Storm? Had Henry come up here? He gave the mare a pat. She nuzzled against him.

Lance found his way back to Blaze and pulled his flashlight from his saddlebag. Holding his revolver in his right hand and the flashlight in his left, he made his way to the mine's entrance.

Ten steps within the crumbling mountain's interior, he transitioned into a stygian darkness far removed from the outside world. The entrance shaft sloped down until he could only stay on his feet if he stooped. He had to be careful stepping in and around remnants of the dusty iron track once used for carts in the mine.

The beam of his flashlight showed areas of runoff and a small pool of standing water to his left. Shards of ice in the water avoided his flashlight beam. Winter still hid in this hole in the ground, bitter and unyielding.

There was a turn ahead to the right. His flashlight beam swept across something, and he swung back to illuminate the toe of a boot before his mind fully processed it. The boot belonged to Henry, who lay unmoving against the hardscrabble rock floor. His body blocked a side shaft. The back wall of the cut-out passageway flickered a faint glow.

Lance sank to his knees and checked his father-in-law. His hands came back bloody. His heart slowed to a timeless ache in his throat, fearing he had been deprived of any chance to tell Alyssa's father how important he was to him and how he had come to love him.

Henry shuddered a long slow breath, and his lashes fluttered open to reveal searching eyes.

"Hang on Henry," urged Lance. "It's me."

Henry reached out to clutch at Lance's shirt.

"Found her," he gasped. "She's here."

Blood frothed at Henry's mouth. He tried to cough and winced. His hand fell back beside him.

"He shot me," said Henry. "Wasn't quick enough."

Lance said, "Who did this to you?"

Henry repeated, "She's here... I found her." His neck muscles corded as he tried to draw in more air.

In the beam of his flashlight, Lance saw Henry's favorite revolver by his side. Somehow his father-in-law had known to look here and interrupted the kidnapper. But where was the girl? And who shot him?

Henry motioned with his hand. Lance moved his face closer. The front of Henry's shirt smelled of gunpowder. Henry reached up and touched Lance's face.

"He took... girl... heard radio... backside... too slow... "

Henry's hand fell to his side, his eyes stilled, and his chest fluttered to a final silence.

Lance knelt beside the only father he had ever known. The rough mine floor cut into his knees. He threw his head back and wanted to scream. He clenched both fists in a fruitless attempt to grasp Henry's spirit and keep him there with him.

He clutched his fists to his chest. Not again, he thought. Everyone he loved, anyone he cared for, gone. He saw Mrs. Lasky's face and heard her questions again, "Who do you see in the mirror? Who do you want to be?"

His father-in-law's last words loomed in his mind. Henry had pleaded for the little girl. He had asked for his help. He would mourn Henry in time, but now he needed to honor him .

Lance rose and shuffled to the end of the side shaft, where he found a hollowed-out space used as a rest station long ago. A folding cot half covered by a ratty old comforter suggested its recent history under the faint glow of a gas lantern on low. Fragments of cut rope lay beside the cot.

He saw scattered boot prints on the dusty rock floor. The glow from the lantern reflected off the hewn walls. A portion of the ceiling had collapsed revealing white quartz and feathery flashes of yellow. Someone had been at that area with tools. He pushed that thought from his mind.

The killer had kept her here. He had come back for her. Maybe he'd heard about the search. But how had Henry known to look here?

He turned and made his way back past Henry's body and noticed an opening on the other side. Another cross shaft.

He searched his flashlight along the opposite shaft as a precaution and sagged to his knees.

Oh God!

His stomach heaved two or three times. He placed both hands on the floor to keep from collapsing. His arms shook. He tried to inhale, but his breath squeezed out through his eyes trying to push away the image of the missing girls arranged in the cross shaft. He was too late for them and wondered if he could ever feel warm again. He knew now. Hell wasn't roasting flames, but a cold and bleak darkness, alone without hope.

Lance stayed there on his hands and knees, tears squeezing out through his clenched eyes and freezing to the tips of his eyelashes. Time passed. Henry's words sounded in his ears along with the roaring certainty that he would never make it back outside.

He visualized Marta. The fourteen-year-old girl had been kept here, bound and terrified. He didn't know how Henry had guessed, but she still had to be close. The teen had not been with the others. He couldn't help the souls trapped in the mine, but Henry had urged him to help the kidnapped girl with his dying breath.

Lance managed a halting gasp of dank, frigid air. He forced himself back to his feet and staggered a few steps, placing his hands against the walls of the shaft to maintain his balance.

He stumbled back out to Blaze and Dot. The two of them stood vigil. Dot's tail thumped the ground. He pulled the radio out of his saddlebag but hesitated. Henry had said the killer heard his voice on the radio. Did that mean he would hear him again if he called for help?

Lance put the radio back in his saddlebag and climbed up on Blaze. The torn earth in front of the mine suggested knobby tire tracks. The killer had used an all-terrain vehicle to get back and forth up here. He must have known justice was closing in. Henry had surprised him. The kidnapper murdered Henry, panicked, and escaped with the girl on an ATV back down the mountain.

Henry told him the kidnapper took Marta down the back way. Lance knew that little used trail circled around and down the mountain and ended close to the Martin farm.

Toward Laura, he realized.

He pulled out his cell phone and tried to call her. No signal.

Lance had been up and down that back-side trail before. There was no way to traverse that trail quickly. It would take the killer time. He listened, but didn't hear any engine noise. He needed to move.

Lightly tapping Blaze with his heels, Lance started down the far side trail. Dot ranged ahead. He focused on his concern for Marta and steeled off his grief for Henry and what he left at the mine.

He searched the trail ahead. He saw Dot show her face through brush on the side of the overgrown trail and vanish to range ahead again. He heard nothing other than the halting clip of the palomino's horseshoes against sliding earth and stone.

Lance thought of the teen girl again. She had to be cold, hungry, and scared out of her mind. He tried not to think of what had likely happened to her.

Please God, he prayed, *let me find her.*

He thought of Laura again and worried. He knew this trail ended at Frank's farm.

Please let her be all right.

Maria Lasky had told him that God hears all prayers even if the answers are hard to hear. She also told him to never lie, even to himself. He knew now that it was all on him. He'd pushed everyone and everything away. He had been afraid of getting hurt again, of losing what he loved.

Like now.

That thought made him sit up in the saddle. He almost lost his balance, but Blaze compensated for his movement. He reached down and patted the stallion.

"What a good horse," he said. "It will be all right. We'll find her. We have to, boy, right?"

Blaze whinnied in response. The stallion was sweating. The footing was uneven and treacherous, and they were pushing hard. Lance saw Dot ahead, circling something on the ground. It looked like a bundle or maybe a... his heart sank. Please no, he thought.

When he reached it, Lance exhaled his relief to see it was a backpack and a blanket. Discarded in the killer's haste to escape, he thought.

After what seemed forever, they reached more open ground at the bottom of the trail. He let Blaze quicken his pace to a trot. Dot raced raced ahead without barking. What a good dog, he thought.

They emerged from the tree line to see the wire fence marking the rear of Frank Martin's farm. A dozen Black Angus cattle lounged under a copse of cottonwood trees in the fading afternoon light. He could see Frank's barn and farmhouse several hundred yards ahead. Nothing looked amiss at first glance.

He checked his cell phone again and found a weak signal. He called both Laura's cell phone and Frank Martin's house phone. There was no answer.

Dot sat expectantly about thirty yards to his right. He walked Blaze over and saw knobby tire tracks in a bare spot on the ground.

"Good girl, Dot. Let's find her."

The shepherd raced ahead, sniffing here and there, following the curve of the property fence line to the right. There was enough room for an ATV to stay between the trees and the fence. He saw fresh tire tracks from time to time.

He slowed to maneuver Blaze around a Rocky Mountain juniper growing close to the fence line. Coming around the tree, he saw Dot sitting ahead looking at him expectantly.

He looked up and saw the cooling ATV next to a gray white van parked amidst a group of quaking aspens.

Lance guided Blaze closer.

The muffler on the ATV appeared to be wrapped with a dark dense foam. The back of the van was open. Loading ramps extended to the ground.

Lance walked Blaze slowly around the empty van.

He looked at the house ahead and to his left. He searched the surrounding trees to his right. If the van was for the ATV, then why hadn't the killer left?

Then Lance saw that the van's left front tire was flat.

CHAPTER ELEVEN

Lance opened the front door of Frank's house to find Laura tending to a shivering Marta in the sitting room. The hypothermic teenager lay on the sofa. The teen's incoherent mumbling betrayed how badly the delirious girl needed medical attention.

Dot padded over to the disheveled teenager and lay her head on the sick girl.

Laura looked at him with wide eyes. Her pupils were maximally dilated.

"Wayne said you'd be on the run by now," she said.

Lance looked around and said, "Where is he?"

She answered him in a ratcheted, tight voice. "He... he went to the garage to pull out my car. He said we needed to get Marta to the hospital."

Lance looked out the window. He saw no sign of the deputy or Laura's car.

"He said he found her on your property in the old mine," said Laura.

She sounded distant, almost resigned. The way she looked at him, he never wanted to have her look at him like that again. She pressed another blanket around Marta, who hadn't stopped shivering.

"I don't understand," she said.

Lance could only imagine what Laura thought. He had burst in on her desperate and furiously determined. He took one step toward her.

"I need you to listen to me," he said.

She started to say something, but another man's voice interrupted. Deputy Wayne Stevens emerged from the doorway behind her.

"No Laura, don't listen to him," said Wayne. "He's dangerous. He's a killer. You know what happened back in Kansas City."

The deputy kept himself lined up behind Laura and the teen.

Lance had no shot.

"Laura," said Wayne. "I've got your car pulled up behind the house. We can get Marta to the hospital. We can save her."

Wayne held his right hand close to the holstered service weapon at his hip.

Lance saw the madness in the deputy's eyes. He needed to keep talking and look for any advantage.

"It's too late for you, Wayne. I've got the radio on VOX," he said. Lance shifted slowly to show the radio attached to his belt at his back left hip. "Everyone can hear you. Everyone knows now." He turned again slowly so that Wayne could see the deputy star pinned to his shirt. "You're under arrest, Wayne."

Wayne's eyes narrowed. He smirked the same soulless smile Lance had seen once before.

"You mean everyone on the radio has heard me trying to save these girls from you," said Wayne.

"Laura, listen to me," said Lance. "Wayne is the killer. I tracked him from the mine. He took Marta. He took Alyssa. He took others, too. He killed Henry at the mine today."

He saw his words pierce her confusion. She gasped. She turned her head to look at Wayne and back at him.

"Don't believe him, Laura," said Wayne. "You don't know him. You know me. You've known me since we were young. Remember." Wayne pitched his voice low and soothing.

Lance imagined that same voice cajoling and manipulating and lying all these years. He knew if they searched carefully enough there would be others that no one knew about.

"Laura, think about this," he said. "Alyssa always knew there was something odd about Wayne. She told me so herself. You told me you used to share secrets. I bet she said something to you. He's been building up to this for years. Look at Marta. She looks like a younger version of you. Please trust me."

Laura looked at him, and her eyes pleaded with him to convince her.

Lance kept his eyes on Wayne. He held his right hand at his side in ready position. He knew he didn't have a chance. Wayne held the local record for speed draw. Henry would now be forever second. He quieted his mind and visualized his right hand ready to draw and sight and stroke the trigger.

"Laura, I love you," said Lance.

Her mouth opened slightly to match her wide eyes, and her right hand came up to her throat.

Dot growled and leaped over Laura just as Wayne's right hand blurred his pistol up and out in a shooting stance.

Lance pulled his revolver better than he ever had, but he knew he wouldn't be fast enough.

He saw Laura lay over Marta and shield the girl with her body.

Wayne had his pistol leveled and was taking up the slack on the trigger when Dot lunged. His service semi-auto discharged striking the shepherd collie who yelped and fell to the floor. The deputy took hold of the pistol with his left hand for his second shot.

Lance noted in the back of his mind how Wayne's perfect form revealed his dedicated practice. His own brain processed front site and press. The rest of his draw leveled out with hammer cocked back and trigger squeeze without conscious thought. He felt the revolver buck in his hand. He saw the look of surprise on the deputy's face at the impact of the heavy .44 caliber slug which slammed into his chest and threw him back against the doorframe.

Deputy Wayne Stevens spent his last moments before eternity searching to make sense of what had just happened. His eyes pleaded a question and widened in fear at the answer fast approaching. He turned to run away and crumpled to the floor.

Lance moved forward and kicked Wayne's pistol out of reach. Only then did he realize the deputy would never reach for it again.

He heard a whimper from Dot. She lay on the floor bleeding. Lance pulled the fabric cover off a nearby chair with shaking hands and pressed it to her wound. Another pair of hands joined him, and Laura kept pressure on his dog's wound. He tried to think through his panic over Dot's pleading eyes. He needed to hurry.

Lance bundled Marta and carried her out to Laura's car idling behind the house. He called on the sheriff's radio but received no reply on his way back into the house to find Laura bundling up Dot. He gathered his dog up and gently carried her to the car on shaky legs. "I'll drive," he said and took the wheel.

Laura sat in the back to apply pressure to Dot's wound and watch over Marta.

"Hurry," she said, her face white.

Lance thought of his phone again. He pulled it out and tossed it back to her and said, "See if you can reach anyone."

He heard Laura get through to Frank. She didn't explain everything, only that they had the girl and were rushing to the clinic. She hung up the phone.

"Frank promised to get Doc Boone," she said.

In the rear-view mirror, he saw her worried look at Marta who had lapsed unresponsive.

Laura prayed out loud, "Please God, let us be in time."

Later, Marta left in a transfer ambulance wrapped in multiple blankets and her grateful parent's love to the neighboring county hospital in Flores Lindas. Doc Boone felt she had a good chance.

The eccentric veterinarian had been more cautious about Dot. He had to operate to repair the damage from the 9mm pistol round, and it would be touch and go overnight.

Sheriff Pullman stood in front of Lance and Laura. He had his hat in hand. A crowd of townspeople crowded into Doc Boone's waiting room behind him.

"I just want to thank you for saving that little girl's life," said Pullman. "I never would have thought... "

The gray haired sheriff trailed off talking and brought his hand up to hide his face and eyes. Several of the onlookers reached out to steady him and pat him on the back.

Sheriff Pullman straightened his shoulders and extended his arm to shake Lance's hand. There were others in the crowd who wanted to shake Lance's hand too, but the sheriff hustled the crowd of onlookers outside. Pullman returned a few moments later.

Lance remembered to ask, "What about Ronnie?"

The sheriff had his hat in hand. "Turns out Ronald Everett couldn't be found because he's been in jail in New Mexico for the last three months for a DUI conviction," said Pullman. He shook his head. "My own deputy. He grew up here. I can't believe it."

"Sociopaths are really good at hiding in plain sight," said Lance. He unpinned the deputy badge on his shirt and tried to give it back to the sheriff.

"Why don't you hold on to that for now," said Pullman, pushing the badge back into Lance's hand. "You're still on the clock."

The sheriff quietly told Lance he would take care of Henry and process the crime scenes at the mine and Frank's house. "Stop by the office in the morning and write up a report detailing everything that happened, okay?"

Lance told Bill he would be at the office in the morning and remembered to mention Storm. The sheriff promised to retrieve Henry's horse and walked out to talk with the rest of the town and a growing number of reporters.

Lance sat in Doc Boone's waiting room on a cushioned bench next to Laura, unable to move or think. That's when he broke down. Laura held him while he sobbed and sobbed, unable to speak. Flash images of the arranged remains in the mine flooded their way to the forefront of his conscious attention, each drowning and calling for help in the maelstrom of his thoughts. He knew he would be seeing them for the rest of his life.

Henry had told him she was there. Somehow, he had suspected Wayne and must have guessed he might have taken her to the mine. Did he mean Marta, or did he see Alyssa? His daughter had been there, displayed in the tomb of that cross shaft along with the others. He hoped Henry would never know. Or maybe he would? He wasn't so sure anymore.

He remembered leaving Blaze tied outside the Martin house and started to get up, but Laura laid a hand on his arm and reminded him that Frank had already taken charge of Blaze and had the magnificent palomino in good care for the night. "He'll look after him and the rest of Henry's horses," she said.

They sat there.

She leaned into him, and said, "Lance, I told you Alyssa wrote me last year."

He nodded that he remembered.

"She helped me escape a bad situation. She was good like that. She made me promise to come out here when I could. She wrote me that I had to meet you."

Lance's vision blurred at her words. It was all too much.

But Laura wasn't finished. "Alyssa wrote me that she couldn't explain, but if anything happened to her, that I needed to find you. She wrote that you would need saving. But I didn't call her right away. I wrote her, but I never got a reply. I should... should have come sooner. I didn't even know until you came to dinner. I..." Her voice trailed off and her tears came hard and fast.

Lance wrapped his arms around her and held her to him. "It was never your fault," he said. "You couldn't have known. None of us realized... " He wasn't sure what to say.

Lance held Laura and thought about Alyssa's last words on the phone. Had she suspected something? Was that what she wanted to talk with him about? He would probably never know. He sat on the bench holding Laura. Her head rested on his shoulder. He could smell the shampoo scent in her hair. They fell asleep for a little while holding on to each other.

In the wee hours of the night, just before dawn, Doc Boone found them. "Dot has a good chance to pull through," he said. "I'd like to hold on to her for several days to be sure."

Lance shook his hand, and Laura hugged the crusty old veterinarian, much to his delight.

Later that morning, Laura sat beside Lance in the sheriff's office until he finished his written summary. She had already given her statement. Both of them were too tired to move, but he still had to get her home. He remembered they only had her car, so maybe Laura would need to get him home.

Soon, they were sitting in her car in their dirty blood-stained clothes, too exhausted to drive home.

She sat behind the steering wheel, sighed, and said, "We're not going anywhere until you tell me again."

"I don't know what you are talking about," he said, almost with a straight face.

She hit him in the arm. It hurt.

Lance looked at Laura. He'd been taught to never lie, especially to himself.

"I'm in love with you," he said, reaching out for her hand.

She didn't let go all the way home.

CHAPTER TWELVE

Lance woke to the sound of birds singing outside his window. Sunlight sprayed inside the room through the white lace decorative under curtains. He yawned and stretched. He shifted out of bed trying not to make too much noise.

Padding out to the bathroom, he washed his face in hot water and shaved. He walked into the kitchen to set the kettle on for oatmeal and tea. Dot raised her head to note his presence and thumped her tail once or twice. She seemed to need more sleep since her injury. He didn't begrudge her that.

He had a lunch sack in the refrigerator with his sandwich, pretzels, and carrot sticks. After lacing up his boots, he donned his work shirt to run out to the barn. Dot followed him. She never passed up a chance to see Blaze.

The palomino lowered his head for his obligatory pats and rubs and proceeded to horse kiss Lance on the side of his face. Dot stretched up to put her front paws on the stall divider. Blaze nuzzled the dog, whose tail wagged in propeller fashion. Lance made sure Blaze received a flake of hay and a morning oats ration. He didn't neglect Storm in the second stall. The sleek black-coated mare missed Henry, but she was adapting well.

On the way back from the barn, he stopped by the henhouse. The girls came strutting out, happy to see him. He threw down some pellets for them, and they all rushed to get their share. Dot sat in the grass outside the chicken coop waiting for him to finish and followed him back to the house. Lance carried six eggs as a reward for his care.

He finished his oatmeal, rinsed out the bowl, and put it in the sink, then changed shirts. Dot finished her morning ration of kibble and followed him back out to the porch. He sipped his tea, enjoying the quiet. He would need to head into work soon.

Lance thought about Henry's Feed Store. That was under control with Frank and Matt. The boy had proved to have a real head for the store and had plans for a business degree. Frank needed the easier work and already thought of Matt as his new grandson.

The screen door opened, and Laura stepped out. She leaned into him and said, "Good morning."

Lance kissed her beautiful face. "Good morning to you. How are you feeling?"

She smiled and said, "No nausea this morning." She had a cup of peppermint leaf tea in her hand.

Dot sat next to Laura, pressing against her legs. She reached down to scratch the shepherd's ears.

"I need to get going," said Lance. "Don't want to be late for my first day."

She kissed him again. "You'll be fine," she said. "Bill has complete faith in you. Just be careful. Promise?"

"Always," said Lance. "See you tonight."

He buckled on his duty belt and stepped down from the porch. He turned to see her standing there. From this angle, he could see that she was beginning to show.

He called out to his dog, "Dot, you watch over her for me?"

The shepherd cocked her head to the side and yipped once.

Climbing into his duty Bronco, he checked that he had everything for work, then adjusted his rearview mirror. For a moment, the angle reflected the six pointed star pinned to his shirt and his name tag, Sheriff Lance Kenyon.

He waved to his family, backed up, and turned down the driveway, his mind busy with his duties for the day. He hoped Bill and Frank didn't drive each other crazy at the Feed Store. The newly retired sheriff needed something to occupy himself, and needling Frank seemed to be his new favorite pastime.

Lance wanted to stop by the gravesite today. The headstones were finished. Henry and Alyssa were buried together next to her mother. He wanted to leave some flowers and say a prayer. They had taken him in and loved him. They were taking care of him still.

His new family would need security. A lawman's salary only went so far. He thought about their child on the way. Laura had plans for their little place, and Frank seemed certain that Blaze might be the key to a horse herd the envy of anyone in the state.

Henry had left the feed store operation to Lance. Hopefully, that would all work out, if he didn't get in the way of his good ideas as Mrs. Lasky would have said.

He reached into his pocket and fingered the nugget from the mine. The assay had come back nearly pure from the sample test he had performed. He had told no one. He wasn't sure he would. Maybe someday.

For now, God would provide.

***

ACKNOWLEDGMENTS

I'm grateful to my beta readers: Phillip, Rachel, Michael, Kathleen, and Stephanie. You made this book better with your excellent feedback.

Thank you Marcelle Cooper for your outstanding copy edit.

Thank you Les (German Creative) for your wonderful cover artwork.

ABOUT THE AUTHOR

Lawrence Simpson is an emerging author of Science Fiction Romance and Romantic Thrillers. This novella is intended as a pleasant diversion for an afternoon or evening. The author can be reached at Lawrence.Simpson@lawrencesimpsonwrites.com

Please consider visiting the author's website at www. lawrencesimpsonwrites.com

Leaving a review at your retailer of choice is always appreciated.

Peace be with you.

ALSO BY LAWRENCE SIMPSON

www.ingramcontent.com/pod-product-compliance
Lightning Source LLC
Chambersburg PA
CBHW020642130626
46552CB00003B/1367